W9-CDD-176

A Note to Parents and Caregivers:

Read-it! Readers are for children who are just starting on the amazing road to reading. These beautiful books support both the acquisition of reading skills and the love of books.

The RED LEVEL presents familiar topics using common words and repeating sentence patterns.

The BLUE LEVEL presents new ideas using a larger vocabulary and varied sentence structure.

The YELLOW LEVEL presents more challenging ideas, a broad vocabulary, and wide variety in sentence structure.

The GREEN LEVEL presents more complex ideas, an extended vocabulary range, and expanded language structures.

When sharing a book with your child, read in short stretches, pausing often to talk about the pictures. Have your child turn the pages and point to the pictures and familiar words. And be sure to reread favorite stories or parts of stories.

There is no right or wrong way to share books with children. Find time to read with your child, and pass on the legacy of literacy.

Adria F. Klein, Ph.D.
Professor Emeritus
California State University
San Bernardino, California

Managing Editors: Bob Temple, Catherine Neitge
Creative Director: Terri Foley
Editor: Jerry Ruff
Editorial Adviser: Mary Lindeen
Designer: Melissa Kes
Page production: Picture Window Books
The illustrations in this book were rendered digitally.

Picture Window Books
5115 Excelsior Boulevard
Suite 232
Minneapolis, MN 55416
877-845-8392
www.picturewindowbooks.com

Printed in the United States of America.

Library of Congress Cataloging-in-Publication Data
Blair, Eric.
Puss in Boots: a retelling of the Grimms' fairy tale / by Eric Blair; illustrated by Todd Ouren.
p. cm. — (Read-it! readers fairy tales)
Summary: An easy-to-read retelling of the tale of a clever cat who wins a fortune and the hand of a princess for his master.
ISBN 1-4048-0591-5 (reinforced library binding: alk. paper)
[1. Fairy tales. 2. Folklore–France.] I. Grimm, Jacob, 1785-1863. II. Grimm, Wilhelm, 1786-1859. III. Ouren, Todd, ill. IV. Puss in Boots. English. V. Title. VI. Series.
PZ8.B5688Pus 2004
398.2'0944'04529752—dc22 2003028244

Puss in Boots

By Eric Blair

Illustrated by Todd Ouren

Special thanks to our advisers for their expertise:
Adria F. Klein, Ph.D.
Professor Emeritus, California State University
San Bernardino, California

Kathleen Baxter, M.A.
Former Coordinator of Children's Services
Anoka County (Minnesota) Library

Susan Kesselring, M.A.
Literacy Educator
Rosemount-Apple Valley-Eagan (Minnesota) School District

Once upon a time, there was a miller who had three sons.

When the miller died, he had only a flour mill, a donkey, and a cat to leave to his sons.

The oldest son got the mill. The second son took the donkey. The youngest son was stuck with the cat, named Puss.

The youngest son was sad. "My brothers can work together to make a living, but what can I do?" he cried. "Surely I will starve."

To the young man's surprise, Puss spoke. "Don't be sad. Having a cat is luckier than you think. Get me a bag and a pair of boots, and I'll show you what I can do for you."

The man knew Puss was clever at catching mice, so he did not doubt him. He did as Puss asked. Puss pulled on the boots and slung the bag over his shoulder.

Puss went off to a rabbit hole.

He opened the bag and placed some bran inside. Then he sat very still.

Soon a rabbit came by. He was curious to know what was in the bag. As soon as the foolish rabbit crawled in to find out, Puss snapped the bag shut.

Puss took the bagged rabbit to the king's palace. "I have a present for His Majesty," he told the guards. In the throne room, Puss gave the rabbit to the king.

"Your Majesty, the Marquis of Calabas told me to bring you this rabbit," he said. The king was happy. But there was no Marquis of Calabas. Puss had made up the name.

Next, Puss trapped some birds.
He went back to the palace and
gave the birds to the king.

The king was so happy, he ordered the cat to be taken down into the kitchen and given something to eat.

One day, Puss knew the king would be driving by the river with his daughter. “Do as I tell you,” Puss told the miller’s son. “Go swimming in the river, and your fortune will be made.”

When the king and his daughter passed the river, Puss cried, “Help! My lord, the Marquis of Calabas, is drowning!” The king told his guards to save the marquis.

While the guards pulled the marquis from the river, Puss told the king that thieves had stolen his master's clothes while he was swimming. The king told his guards to bring a fine suit for the marquis.

The miller's son put on the suit. He was so handsome that the king's daughter convinced her father to let the miller's son ride in the carriage with them.

Puss marched ahead. He passed some workers in a field. He cried, "Good people! Here comes the king. If you do not tell him that this field belongs to the Marquis of Calabas, you will all be killed."

When the king's carriage drove by, the king asked the workers, "Who owns this field?" The frightened workers answered, "The Marquis of Calabas."

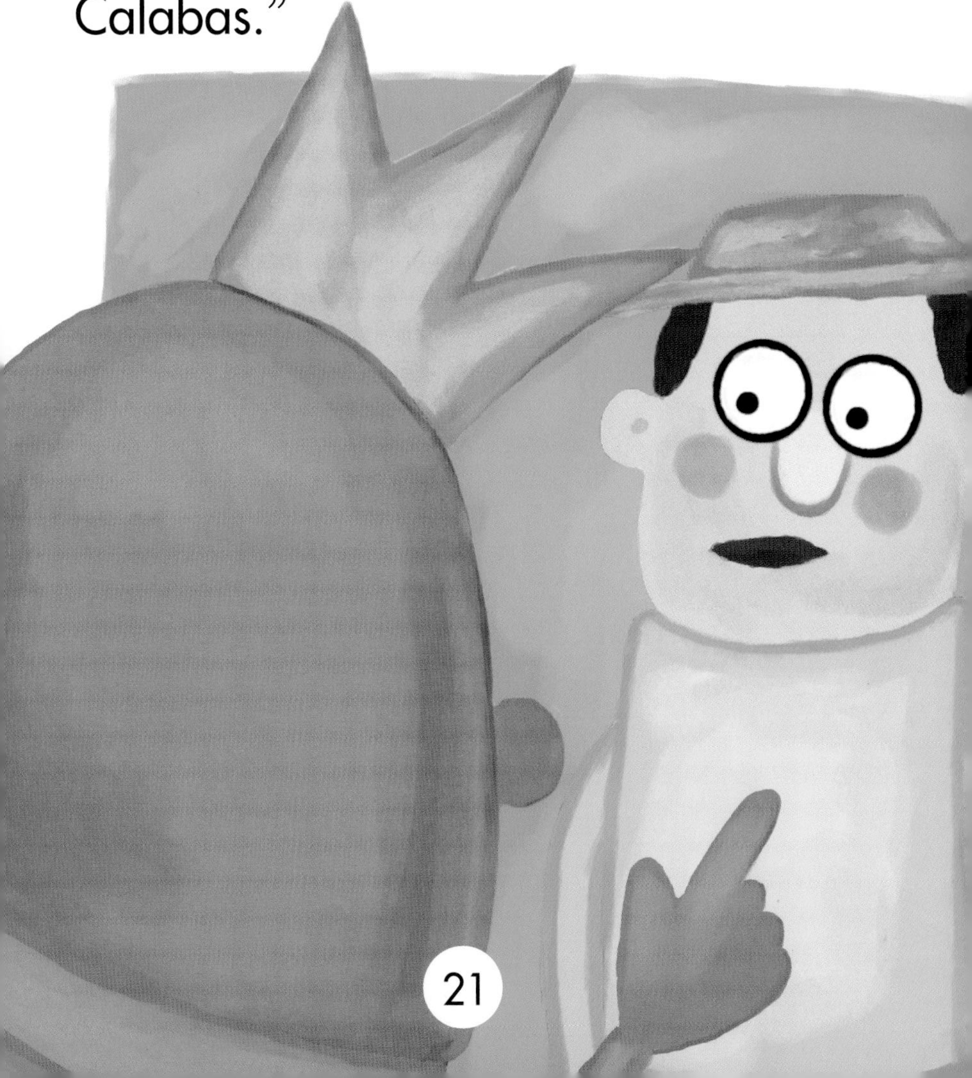

In the next field, workers were harvesting wheat. “The king is coming,” said Puss. “If you do not tell him this wheat belongs to the marquis, you will be chopped up!” So the king learned that this field also belonged to the marquis.

Finally, Puss came to a castle. Inside lived an ogre. The ogre owned all the land through which the king had passed. Puss told the ogre's servants that he wanted to meet the ogre, and they let him in.

"People tell lies about you," Puss said to the ogre. "They say you can change yourself into any animal you please."

"It's true," said the ogre. Then he changed into a lion.

“But they say you can take the shape of a mouse,” Puss said. “Surely that is impossible.”

“Impossible?” cried the ogre. “I’ll show you!” But no sooner had the ogre changed himself into a mouse than Puss pounced on him and ate him up.

The king's carriage soon stopped at the ogre's castle. Puss greeted the king. "Welcome to the castle of my lord, the Marquis of Calabas."

The king asked, "This belongs to the marquis, too?"

The miller's son took the king and his daughter into the castle. In the dining hall, they found the tables had been set with a delicious dinner. They had a great feast.

Both the king and the princess were charmed with the marquis. Finally, the king said, “Marquis, I would be very happy if you would become my son-in-law.”

The miller's son took one look at the beautiful princess and agreed. He and the princess were married that very day and lived happily ever after.

Puss became a great lord, too.
He never again chased mice,
except for fun.

Levels for *Read-it!* Readers

Read-it! Readers help children practice early reading skills with brightly illustrated stories.

Red Level: Familiar topics with frequently used words and repeating patterns.

Blue Level: New ideas with a larger vocabulary and a variety of language structures.

Little Red Riding Hood by Maggie Moore
The Three Little Pigs by Maggie Moore

Yellow Level: Challenging ideas with an expanded vocabulary and a wide variety of sentences.

Cinderella by Barrie Wade
Goldilocks and the Three Bears by Barrie Wade
Jack and the Beanstalk by Maggie Moore
The Three Billy Goats Gruff by Barrie Wade

Green Level: More complex ideas with an extended vocabulary range and expanded language structures.

The Brave Little Tailor by Eric Blair
The Bremen Town Musicians by Eric Blair
The Emperor's New Clothes by Susan Blackaby
The Fisherman and His Wife by Eric Blair
The Frog Prince by Eric Blair
Hansel and Gretel by Eric Blair
The Little Mermaid by Susan Blackaby
The Princess and the Pea by Susan Blackaby
Puss in Boots by Eric Blair
Rumpelstiltskin by Eric Blair
The Shoemaker and His Elves by Eric Blair
Snow White by Eric Blair
Sleeping Beauty by Eric Blair
The Steadfast Tin Soldier by Susan Blackaby
Thumbelina by Susan Blackaby
Tom Thumb by Eric Blair
The Ugly Duckling by Susan Blackaby
The Wolf and the Seven Little Kids by Eric Blair

A complete list of _Read-it!_ Readers is available on our Web site: www.picturewindowbooks.com